Mister MAGGS

Piccadilly Pips

Mister MAGGS

Helen Cresswell

Illustrated by Jamie Smith

Piccadilly Press • London

Phototypeset by Piccadilly Press.
Printed and bound in Hong Kong by Colorcraft Ltd.,
for the publishers Piccadilly Press Ltd.,
5 Castle Road, London NW1 8PR

A catalogue record for this book is available from the
British Library

ISBN: 1 85340 342 3

Helen Cresswell lives in a Georgian farmhouse in
Newark, Nottinghamshire. She has written over a
hundred books for children and also writes TV
drama. This is her first for Piccadilly Press.

Jamie Smith lives in Uttoxeter, Staffordshire. He stud-
ied Illustration at De Montfort University, and grad-
uated last year. This is his second book and his first
for Piccadilly Press.

Jemima Pinchin was seven years
old and lived at number twenty-
eight Lime Street. She had an older
brother, Jake, who was a show off,
and a baby brother, Joe, who yelled
a lot. Mrs Pinchin liked names
beginning with the letter J. Mr
Pinchin said it was lucky they
weren't wanting twenty children,
or she would either run out of
names, or end up calling them

names like Jampot or Jellybaby.

As it happened, Jemima's best friend in the whole world was called Jane. The good news was that she lived at number twenty-six Lime Street. The bad news was that her family were moving house.

When the day came Jemima and Jane were in floods of tears. They promised they would save up all their pocket money for stamps so that they could write to one another every single day. They promised they would visit each other in the school holidays.

"I can't bear it!" Jemima wailed. "Oh, she's going, and she's my best friend in the world!"

"Cheer up," said Mr Pinchin. "Plenty more fish in the sea."

"Trust a girl to be a cry baby!"

Jake said.

"Just look at him wave!" cried
Mrs Pinchin, holding Joe high.
"What a clever boy!"

"Nothing clever about waving,"
Jake said, and for once Jemima
agreed with him.

The car turned the corner and disappeared.

"That's that, then!" said Mr Pinchin, and set off up to the shop for a paper.

That was that. This was the worst day in Jemima's whole life and nobody cared. She might as well be invisible for all the notice anyone took.

She turned and trudged back towards the house.

Crack! Whoops! She'd trodden on Joe's rattle, lying by his pram.

"Oh Jemima! *Now* look what you've done!"

"It wasn't me!" Jemima blurted. "Mister Maggs did it!"

She said it before she even had time to think. She didn't know why she said it, she just did. She ran into

the back garden and jumped on the
swing. Everything swam into a
green blur.

"That was funny!" she thought.
"Mister Maggs... Where did *he*
come from? Why's he turned up all
of a sudden. Who is he, anyway?"

Then she knew.
"To be my best friend! To be my
best friend in the whole world now
Jane's gone!"

It must be true. After all, he had turned up out of the blue to take the blame for breaking the rattle. Only a best friend would do that.

"Thanks, Mister Maggs!" she said out loud. "Like a swing?"

She climbed off and began to push the empty swing to and fro.

"You gone potty or what?"

It was Jake, getting his bike from the shed. She stuck out her tongue and carried on pushing. She soon got tired of that, though. She tried to think what games you could play with an invisible friend. She couldn't. Certainly not hide and seek. She decided to pick some flowers and arrange them in Mum's best vase, to make up for the broken rattle.

"See you later, Mister Maggs!"

She picked the best flowers she could find. Then she went to fetch the green vase. It was on the mantel-piece in the living room, and next to it was Mum's favourite ornament, a glass dolphin. Jemima had to stand on tiptoe and stretch... stretch...Whoops! Her fingers slipped and the dolphin wobbled and rocked. Jemima held her breath, and the dolphin wobbled and settled down again. It was a good job. If it had fallen and smashed on the tiled hearth, Jemima thought she might have to leave home.

In the kitchen she found Dad staring at the draining board.

"Those are my prize blooms for the show! Who's picked them!"

Jemima gulped. Her good deed had just turned into a bad deed. "Mister Maggs! Mister Maggs did it!"

He went striding out into the garden to inspect his plants.

"Oh Mister Maggs," said Jemima, "you are naughty!" And she waggled her finger and giggled.

And then it happened. He came out of thin air, he shimmered out of nowhere. Jemima saw a shock of orange hair, a pointy nose and bright green eyes. He was wearing

a baggy suit with red and yellow
checks, with a green shirt and red
and yellow spotted bow tie. He had
twiggy fingers and black shiny
boots.

Jemima stared up at him. He was much bigger than she was. She shut her eyes. Then, slowly and fearfully, she opened them again. Still there! Starting at the shiny boots, her eyes travelled up until they met his. He grinned, and held out his hand as if to shake. Jemima slowly put out her own, then changed her mind and snatched it back.

The door opened and Mum came in. Jemima clapped her hand to her mouth and shut her eyes again, tight.

"Don't stand round under my feet, Jemima. What are all those flowers doing on the draining board?"

"Must have gone," Jemima thought, and opened her eyes. She gasped. Her mother was darting here and there about the kitchen and Mister Maggs was neatly side-stepping. As she passed him to go out again he made a sweeping bow.

"Whew!" Jemima let out a gasp of relief. "She didn't see you!"

Now he was strolling about the kitchen inspecting it. He lifted lids and peered into the cupboard. He dipped his finger into the sugar bowl and licked it. He snatched up the flowers, plonked them in the vase and filled it from the tap.

"Mister Maggs..." Jemima began. He turned. "Why...why exactly have you come here?"

Instead of replying he went out through the back door and into the garden.

"No! Don't! Dad's out there!"

So he was, but he didn't appear to notice Mister Maggs. He seemed to look straight through him.

"Something very peculiar's going on here," thought Jemima Pinchin, who by now had quite forgotten that this was the worst day of her whole life when her best friend in the world had gone away.

In his pram Joe began to bawl. Mister Maggs went over and peered in. He pulled faces, he waggled his fingers. The crying stopped. Jemima could not work it out. Mister Maggs lifted the pram, plucked a flower from right under Mr Pinchin's nose and stuck it in his buttonhole. It clashed horribly with his suit.

"Jemima, run to the shop for me, will you?" Mum was at the back door. "Here's a bag and the money – half a pound of butter, please, we need it for tea and for the picnic tomorrow."

Jemima took the bag and the money and beckoned Mister Maggs to follow her. Once they were safely out of the garden Jemima stopped.

"Why can't Mum and Dad see you?" she asked. "And why don't you *say* something."

A car went by. Mister Maggs waved but no one waved back.

"Can't – can't *anyone* see you except me?"

She would soon find out. PC Cobb was wheeling his bike towards them.

"Oh wow! Now what? Can you be arrested for being invisible?"

Now Mister Maggs was swinging from the wrought iron arch to the churchyard. Could he be arrested for that? She very much hoped not. She was beginning to like the jaunty

Mister Maggs. And if he took the blame for everything she did wrong, she would never be in trouble again for the rest of her life.

He made her very nervous in the shop though. He strolled about, picking things up and putting them down. He pointed at old Mrs Brown's huge flowery hat and rolled his eyes. As they went out, he tipped the OPEN sign on the door to CLOSED with a single deft twitch of a finger.

He pranced back down the street ahead of Jemima, hands in pockets, whistling. He stopped suddenly. There, chalked on the ground, was a hopscotch game. Mister Maggs beamed. He stooped, picked up a stone and rolled it. Next minute Jemima had plonked the shopping

bag on the wall and they were both
playing.

Mister Maggs enjoyed himself
mightily. He leapt and jumped on
his grasshopper legs and waved his
arms to keep his balance. The only

trouble was, he was cheating. Jemima saw him with her own eyes, though she could hardly believe it. If his pebble rolled short of the square he wanted, he merely gave a little snap of his fingers and the pebble moved, of its own accord, into the right square.

This was serious magic. Next time her pebble rolled short, Jemima tried it herself. She didn't really expect it to work, and it didn't.

"Not playing!" she said, and marched crossly off. "You're cheating! And why don't you *say* something? Why don't you talk?"

There was no answer to that. Mister Maggs evidently didn't go in for talking.

Back home Mum was busy in the kitchen.

"You've been a long time," she said. "Where's the butter?"

Whoops! Jemima had put the bag on the wall while she played hop-scotch, and there it still was – or at least, she hoped so.

"Oh – you haven't left it in the shop!"

Jemima thought fast. Before, when she had blamed Mister Maggs, she hadn't known he was there. This time, he was actually watching her. He was wagging his finger and shaking his head. But what harm could it do? He wouldn't get into trouble. No one even knew he was there. She took a deep breath.

"It wasn't my fault! It was Mister Maggs!"

He gave her a look as if to say, "Oh Jemima, what a whopper!" and Mum said, "Who *is* this Mister Maggs," and Jake said, "She's off her rocker!"and Jemima fled to fetch the butter.

Mister Maggs seemed to be in a sulk. He marched ahead of her, and as they drew level with the hopscotch and the wall where the shopping bag was, instead of turning back he kept going. She stared after him, not sure whether to be glad or sorry.

"Mister Maggs! Mister Maggs!"

He showed no sign of hearing. He just kept on going. But at least he didn't disappear, he didn't vanish into thin air. He might be back.

The next day was Jake's birthday and the family was going for a picnic. His favourite present was a beautiful rainbow kite and they were going to find somewhere to fly it. Jemima made a promise to herself that if there was such a thing as being good as gold, she was going to be it – all day. If she didn't do anything to blame Mister Maggs for, perhaps he wouldn't turn up. On the other hand, she couldn't be sure.

When the family set off in the car there had been no sign of him.

"He must have gone back to where he came from," Jemima thought. "Wherever that is."

They found a perfect place to fly the kite. The car was unloaded, out came the rugs and chairs, the bat and ball and kite. Jemima helped to put

out the food. First she spread the rug.
Then, when no one was looking, she
unscrewed a thermos and had a
secret swig of orange juice. She
peered into a bag and saw egg and
cress sandwiches which were her
favourite. Should she pinch one?
Promises, promises, Jemima Pinchin.
Who was going to be as good as
gold?

She took one. It was half way to her lips when a twiggy hand appeared out of the blue and snatched it. Jemima jumped and whirled round. She kicked the thermos and orange juice spilled all over the rug.

"Jemima!"

"Oh *now* look what you've done!"

Jemima hesitated. Mister Maggs, mouth full of egg sandwich, was frowning at her and shaking his head as if to warn her. But she took no notice.

"It wasn't me! Mister Maggs did it!"

He gave her a long, thoughtful stare. Then he wove his way between the rest of the family who were busy rescuing the food from the rug. He picked up the kite, the beautiful rainbow kite, and started to run with it. No one saw him but Jemima.

She ran after him, but by the time she reached him the kite was already up and flying. Jemima jumped and tried to pull the string from his grasp, but he laughed wickedly and the kite went higher still.

"Jemima!"

"Hey! My kite!"

Jake and Dad came running.

"Oh please, please!" Jemima gasped. But Mister Maggs, with a gleeful smirk, tugged the string from her grasp – and let go! He watched for a moment as the kite went sailing up into a high tree, then stuck his hands in his pockets and sauntered off.

Poor Jemima! Now it was her turn to take the blame for something she hadn't done.

"It was Mister Maggs, it was

Mister Maggs!" she screamed, and for
once she was telling the truth. But no
one believed her. Why should they?
They had seen her flying the kite
with their own eyes – or thought they
had.

Jemima Pinchin had a terrible time after that. She had invented Mister Maggs and now she couldn't shake him off. He appeared and disappeared. Sometimes he followed her like her own shadow. And he thought of far worse things to get up to than ever she could.

For a start, he changed the time on the clock in the kitchen. He let down both tyres on Jake's bike, he put out his foot and tripped Jemima up when she was carrying a plate of food. He put the plug in the washbasin, squirted in bubble bath and turned both taps on full.

And Jemima got all the blame. She could tell them that Mister Maggs did it till she was blue in the face, but she still had her pocket money stopped and was sent to bed early.

"Oh please, please stop it!" she
begged him. "I'm sorry I blamed you,
I really am!"

But never a word did he say in
reply.

Then, one day, Jemima was sitting
at the table doing a jigsaw puzzle and
Mister Maggs was wandering about
the room, fingering things, plumping

cushions, switching lights on and off.
He sauntered over to the mantelpiece
and tipped the glass dolphin with a
finger and it began to rock.

"Oh no! Not that! Please don't!"

He looked at her very long and
hard and then, with a smile, tipped
the dolphin again.

Crash! Down it fell to the tiled
hearth and smashed to smithereens.
Next minute Mum and Jake were
there and they looked at the dolphin
and then Jemima, and she looked at
Mister Maggs.

He nodded. Now she knew what
she must do. She took a very deep

breath, then ran towards her mother.

"I did it! Oh Mum, I'm sorry – I did it!"

Mister Maggs was beaming. And then it happened. He faded. The orange hair and gaudy suit went into a thin rainbow blur and then he had gone! Jemima didn't know whether to laugh or cry. He had, after all, been magic, and there wasn't much of that about at number twenty-eight Lime Road.

"You sure that Mister Maggs didn't do it?" Jake was saying.

"Oh no," said Jemima. "I did."

"Well, never mind," said Mum. "And thank goodness we've heard the last of that Mister Maggs. Look out of the window, Jemima, and see what's happening."

So she looked out and saw a big

furniture van outside number twenty
-six, and standing by it was a girl of
about her own age. She turned and
looked straight at Jemima and
Jemima waved and the girl waved
back.

"Hurray! I bet her name begins with J!" said Jemima.

Soon she had a new best friend called Julie Green and sometimes she would wonder whether she had Mister Maggs to thank. He had, after all, been a friend – sort of.

JIMMY JELLY
by Jacqueline Wilson

"I KNOW he's not on the telly," says Angela. "He's squeezed out of that boxy bit at the back of the telly and he's come to visit me."
"Oh yes?" I say. "So where is he then? I can't see him."
"Of course YOU can't see," says Angela. "I'm the only one that can see him because he's MY Jimmy Jelly."

Rosie and Mum hate Jimmy Jelly's television programme. But they hate him even more when he's there – with Angela – all the time. Then the REAL Jimmy Jelly comes to the Shopping Centre and everybody's in for a surprise...

THE MUCKITUPS
by Robert Swindells

Opposites certainly don't attract when the Muckitups move in next door to the Frimlys! The Frimlys are really tidy; the Muckitups are, well, mucky. When their muckiness spreads into the garden the Frimlys are furious!

"The tidy, healthy, Hebridean Frimlys clash then mix with the junk-strewing, chain-smoking, telly-watching Muckitups!" – The Times

THE CAR-WASH WAR
by Andrew Matthews

Trees has to admit that her ghastly twin, Tel, and
his friend have come up with a fantastic idea for
earning loads of money!
But she and Yasmin soon argue with the founders
of the Arnhem Street Car-Wash Company and set
up the rival Santa Car-Wash!
Chaos breaks out as they all find ever more
ingenious ways to win business.